TO KNEW BEGINNINGS

Veil of Shadows

DAVID S. MUNCY

To Knew Beginnings: Veil of Shadows
David S. Muncy © 2025

Because of the dynamic nature of the Internet, any web addresses or links contained in this book may have changed since publication and may no longer be valid. The views expressed in this work are solely those of the author and do not necessarily reflect the views of the publisher, and the publisher hereby disclaims any responsibility for them.

Paperback: 978-1-952648-82-3
Hardcover: 978-1-952648-83-0

CONTENTS

CHAPTER TWENTY-ONE

"Oh Hayden."

CC talked softly. Hayden was just waking up and he heard her voice again and felt like a fool. He had come all the way to Waverly Hall with the group that was escorting CC to Hasson Heights, and had become aware of just how interesting and refreshing it could be just to have a beautiful young woman at his side again.

She was so much sweeter than he expected. They had become fast friends, bosom buddies even, and Hayden was very glad that she decided to reenter the world as he had. The shrewish voice he had heard was gone. He actually felt like a grandfather with his favorite granddaughter for company, and it just meant the world to him that he had found a friend in such a sweet young lady.

That didn't mean she was always sweet. When he first joined her caravan, she was just as obnoxious and mean as he had expected. What he didn't expect was that first night she had come to him. He didn't know what to expect when she stopped by like she had, just walking straight into the enclosure he had brought along for the journey. They were traveling like wealthy merchants and seeing her duck when she walked into his new home on the road, he realized she was young, beautiful, and scared.

Standing there looking at her he could just imagine the trepidation that she was feeling. With a sad smile, Hayden held his hand out, wanting to see what her reaction would be. It was a sobering moment for in that instant he felt a need to protect her come over him so strongly that he just motioned for her to come to him and said, "You're afraid aren't you, love."

That is when the façade cracked and she nodded briefly, and he saw a tear run down her cheek, breaking his heart to think of the courage this young woman must have just to be where she was, at her age, having to wait patiently for so long, just to be flung into a journey that could very well end in pain and misery. That is if Hasson Heights and Waverly Hall did go to war as he expected them to.

After that first night together, it became routine for CC to put the elderly Hayden to bed and see to it that he had his breakfast each morning. She simply told him that it was not work if it was something you loved, and explained to him that she just had a need to take care of someone. The shrewish voice was just a mechanism she used to avoid temptation and to push away any thought other than what her father expected.

She was a brood mare, she said, but Hayden could see right away after that night, first of just listening to the young woman as she lowered her voice and just opened her heart to him. He was surprised, somewhat, though he was warned this would happen. It was just a shock after his first impression of her that he felt very protective and realized that she was even more than she seemed to be on first sight. That was a lot in itself, and he was determined to see the match through, and actually had penned a letter that was being delivered in haste to Clayton's father, explaining the situation the young woman was in and his desire to help.

Hayden was not a fighter by any means, so he made use of what skills he had as a teacher in the academy and his insight into the minds of young men and women, as there were women occasionally in class for select purposes. It didn't take long for him to realize that the shrewish voice did make it seem like she was a mare for riding. And she was. There was more, though, and she had an outstanding memory, being able to quote verbatim something she had seen or barely heard years before in a flash without much fuss at all. She really was truly amazing, once she let her guard down, and he knew Clayton would be well pleased. Hopefully he would live long enough to enjoy her. Clayton was in the middle of a mess, and nothing held a guarantee.

Hayden never expected to actually like the woman, much less respect her. She kept her true personality well-hidden and it took him aback to realize she was someone he could simply be friends with, and a guide for, out of simple admiration and respect. She was the granddaughter that he needed, without even knowing that he actually needed someone.

He was almost ashamed of himself for all of the wasted years of teaching, and was apologetic to himself for being so distracted for so long that he actually forgot what life was really all about. He had thought he was intelligent, determined to see the course through, and had just realized that it was foolish pride that had kept him going for so long.

What got him the most was the first time she hugged him and she lightly said, "I miss my dad. We were close. Will you hold me?"

Taken aback by seeing how vulnerable the young lady honestly was made him react slowly. His first impression had been an act and she was just a lost child in the world. It made him feel very protective and realize that he was lost in the world as well.

So, he held her, close, and said, "I am lost too, child, maybe we can learn together?"

CHAPTER TWENTY-TWO

Solara's formation was something she had thought of before, but hadn't had a chance to put into the field. Four of her ranks were carrying just a long spear, angled over the shoulder of the man in front of them, while the very first rank carried swords in the enveloping arms of the multiple spearheads around them, and slowly began a huddled march forward. Clayton was at the outer wall of the side they were advancing to, and had already punched a hole in the defenses of Clendenin.

The catapult had worked wonders and had made two gaping openings that Clayton had been trying to force his men into, that is until Solara had motioned for him to back off and hold steady.

She knew the defenders were reeling from the assault, but just as she suspected, his men were not well trained in taking a fortress, or even a large, defended structure like the outpost.

She felt she had the answer to that. The spears would be guided by the men in front of the wielder and held steady through the lines to keep anyone from advancing to the front line from the enemy. If any were able to breach the spearheads, the lone swordsman from each column would be there to clear them out and make any room needed, being protected on both sides from the advancing blades on the spears.

The dangerous part would be when they entered the defile from the catapult. The swordsmen would have to get through quickly to take a defensive position while the spear holders held the enemy in check as they cleared the area. Solara's men would kill anyone they came into contact with, except Clayton himself.

The new unit that had arrived late brought new orders from the emperor. Solara was told that she would give a demonstration of Emperor Ishima's dedication to the conquering of the new territory, but Clayton must not be harmed. He would be a mouth piece for the clans, and no one else need be hurt, as long as he could understand.

There were other lands that were not connected to the continent that had been exploring around Terlingua. They were a totally unknown entity that had the emperor worried, and she would have to change tactics and take the lead from Clayton but still use him to control the clans for the horsemanship of their armies. It would be a reality check for most everyone. Emperor Ishima had already told Clayton's father that they could help or be eliminated, and this would be the first true test of the commitment that he had made. There was too much going on that was unknown for either to do more than agree to see to Waverly Hall.

The formation moved forward slowly, and she knew it would be an intimidating sight just to see the spearheads once they were lowered. Moving Clayton out of the way was very important, and he must be alive, if not alert, at the end of the battle.

Her men's armor was based on a similar design for everyone. Different accoutrements designated rank, but there would be no change in protection or rank once the battle commenced. Each rank could be identified by the armor's design, which made it easier to find allies in the midst of a battle. The humidity back home forced them to use lacquer for their scales, which was an oddity in this part of the realm.

She was surprised to learn about the agreement between the emperor and Iasson Heights, but had to admit it was a bold move, as anyone could have said no, but the decision from King Justin had been unanimous and decisive. She couldn't blame them for that.

Solara was on horseback, thanks to Clayton, and watched as her men approached the breach. They had already proceeded through Clayton's lines, and the ranks behind the spears had cut a swath through those lines, to make way, so it was awkward keeping the line straight when entering.

The spearmen thrust forward identically, while the few swordsmen balanced lightly in between the shafts protecting them. It was slow going because the lines rose and shifted as they made the entrance through the rubble of the collapsed wall. The spears were constantly shifting as the lone swordsmen from that file negotiated the maze of spearheads that proceeded directly in front of him.

The best chance the swordsman had to live was staying close to his formation while allowing the spearmen behind him to negotiate any resistance from the enemy as they progressed steadily through the breach of the outpost.

Solara watched closely as her men negotiated the defile and did not see anyone falter. Even now she was still amazed by the body control and strength her men possessed. Such a display was harrowing for the enemy, and she was excited seeing such skill on display.

Clayton had been pushed to the side, for his own safety, so Solara walked towards the outpost, looking at the refuse piled up from the defenders attempt to stop Clayton's men from proceeding to enter the breach. The defenders were overrun by the impetus of so many blades pushing through them. Numbers mattered, but the closely packed defenders had nowhere to go other than against a wall or forward with a blade in their chest.

Solara watched as the calculated progress was made through the open grounds of the outpost. It was the most methodical presentation she had witnessed firsthand in all of the battles that she had seen. It made her want to stick her chest out and cheer them on.

Some of Clayton's men had been caught up in the fray of Solara's attack, but most had been able to step aside to make way for the brutal formation steadily advancing. Bewildered, Clayton saw Solara watching her men and noticed a gleam in her eye and a primal excitement spread across her face.

She seemed to be enjoying herself immensely. Clayton's men had punched a hole that made it possible for anyone to advance, but the methodical attack by the monks was a true display of honed precision. They pushed ever forward with a slow gate that was meant to keep the men in line, with the ability to spread to either side once through the breach, and also to their footing so they could not be pushed back.

Solara was duly impressed by her men's performance, even by the standards she had set at home during the civil strife. She was positive that Clayton would see their worth with just this one display and hoped that the other outposts fell just as easily. It would be a full day before anyone knew anything about the other attacks taking place and they had lost some time building the catapult which may have thrown off the timing of some of the attacks.

The defenders had been engaged in the foreground of the outpost where Solara's men began steadily pushing everyone back. Friend or foe didn't matter, and the monks slowly tore into the ranks ahead of them.

Solara could see that she was in control of the field and gave a high-pitched whistle from a device that hung around her neck. Her men were trained to form up and hold their ground at that signal, and she saw her men form up in an aggressive defensive position.

Waiting for new orders, Solara could hear the swordsmen doing their work of disengaging and untangling the lines. She knew they would clear out the enemy and waited until the fighting had stopped before she entered the outpost. Clayton caught on that there was a break in the fighting and headed to the entrance as well, trying to catch up with her.

She knew she would have to explain things to Clayton, but for now she wanted to address her men and the unrivaled ability that had been on display. She chose to walk in the gap between defenders and her men, and she could see the trepidation and hate in the eyes of the defeated enemy.

She would let Clayton decide what to do with those men as this was close to his home, and she was just visiting.

Walking the circumference of the gap between armies, Clayton stood back and saw that some of his own men had been taken out along with the enemy. He could see that his men were outnumbered and in a very vulnerable position, and wanted to yell at Solara but wouldn't do it in front of anyone. Putting a lid on his anger, he simply waited to see what she would do next.

Solara strolled from one end to the other without saying anything. The sounds of birds in the distance made for a nice setting, though the remains of some of the men, and shattered breathing, made it difficult to look at anything else.

Deciding that it was time to let Clayton be master of the field again, she stopped in front of her troops and said, "Clayton, what would you do with these men. I am afraid that there were more casualties than we expected. Some have been your own men. I apologize if we have gone beyond the means of our agreement, but my men were ready for a fight."

Unsure just what to say, Clayton took a moment to wrap his head around the situation, and deciding, said, "I will deal with the prisoners."

Feeling relegated to second best, Clayton gave a small bow and started giving commands to take any weapons that the enemy had and round the men up for his decision.

Solara nodded briefly, in approval it seemed, but she left her men in position, though with a small hand motion the spears were raised, and the men appeared to relax. He was not relaxed at all, nervous even, but he just had to follow through with the necessities of deciding what to do with the men that were left.

The wounded were separated from the healthy, and prisoners were stripped of all but their underclothes. Leaving his men to it, Clayton caught Solara watching him and noticed her men held their position. Somewhat baffled by the actions of the day, Clayton left the outpost to see that a camp for the injured was set up.

CHAPTER TWENTY-THREE

King Justin had just received his first report from Clayton and the battle for Clendenin. The messenger sent also had a private message where Justin heard words that he had been afraid would be uttered once things began.

Clayton simply said that a wolf had been set free. What Clayton did not know of was the agreement that Justin had been subjected to accept from the Emperor of Terlingua. He really hadn't been given much of a choice and was ashamed to tell his son that the monks had threatened the elimination of Hasson Height's if they did not participate in the attacks on Waverly Hall's outposts as a first step to destroying King Simon and all evidence of Waverly Hall's existence.

Justin knew he had overstepped his bounds with Terlingua. He needed a distraction toward Waverly Hall to force everyone's attention to

Waverly Hall again. Clayton must have been shown something during the attack on Clendenin for him to send that message so quickly.

Seldin had walked by Justin after Justin was given that message. It was almost as if Seldin wanted to see his reaction first hand.

Wondering how Seldin could have known, Justin realized the lines of communication among the monks were second to none. For them to just have arrived they most certainly moved quickly.

Clayton was simply outmatched. Accepting the agreement with Emperor Ishima, Justin knew this would occur, but he had hoped it wouldn't have occurred so soon.

He didn't expect to have his own reports until tomorrow eve. He would have all the reports from the attacks on all of the outposts at that time. Not just Clendenin. It seemed Seldin was more concerned about the "Commander Solara" than he was anything else. Justin didn't understand the reasoning for that and decided to just let it go and find out for himself.

After the business with Jonas Weaver at the broken servant, he had opened his mind to wider possibilities through the realm to help stay the onslaught of the monks and build more of his own men. Under Clayton.

He could see the need to reach out to the clans again and this time he would let them know that the monks were allies, but they were a threat also, as they wanted to have a presence on the mainland. No one among Hasson Height's would care for that idea, and it was time to beat the drum and call up more of his own, to see Clayton through the coming battles.

Undeterred, Justin knew before the monks arrived that there would be some type of confrontation. He hadn't anticipated it being during their first attack. He hated to admit it but he was not prepared. Clayton would be the one to suffer because of that.

There was also the matter of Jonas Weaver. That had been an ordeal and he was glad to put it behind him. It did bring up another set of problems, with Waverly Hall, as he knew that they knew Hasson Height's was preparing for war. And Waverly Hall would respond.

The question he wanted answered was would the monks contain themselves or would they engage Waverly Hall and his own men. He was afraid the monks would turn against everyone as almost happened in Clendenin.

He felt that Emperor Ishima may have been overly confident when Justin agreed to ally with the monks for an attack on Waverly Hall. By Solara's action that Clayton reported on, Justin was ready to turn all of the clansmen armor against them.

It could very well end up with no one to have an ally to rely on, and Clayton was stuck right in the middle of it.

It seemed this Solara was the best the monks had and his shock troops made quite the impression. He was dangerous, and Justin knew Solara would push things as far as he dared to gain reputation on the mainland.

Pride was a weakness in the monks, but he wasn't sure how to exploit it. At the moment Clayton was outnumbered in the field, and Justin regretted that happened. It didn't fit in well with the business of Jonas Weaver either. It could be the monks playing both sides so they would eliminate each other.

There was too much on the line for silliness like that. It must be Solara's way of making a statement, and Clayton had confirmed that loud and clear. He would have to invigorate the chiefs to call more men forward, as a secondary force. He would try to hold them close enough to the fray to be known but far enough away to be a distant threat. That would send a clear message, rather than Clayton having to hunker down and just take whatever the fates threw at him.

It was such a damn mess, and the monks were somehow dominating thoroughly as soon as there was an engagement. Justin would have to redo his due diligence concerning the campaign against Wavery Hall. A simple aggressive act would be enough to push Waverly Hall into attack and with the short explanation of how aggressive the monks were with Clayton it looked like that was beyond repair. That is what was expected with the attack, though, so it was a fine line this Solara was walking.

Justin felt things were advancing too quickly. Now, too, that Solara had another three thousand men at his back, Justin was worried. He wasn't sure what he had unleashed on the mainland, much less just Hasson Heights. With the agreement he had made there really wasn't much he could do.

Now he was worried that Clayton would survive with so many powerful influences acting at once. Justin new he must act. Tired of waiting for the other reports, Justin stood in his study and decided to send word for help from the other clans.

This was his move to solidify his claim asking for the support to see the struggle through.

He doubted anyone would object, but it was a possibility. His hold as king was tenuous, simply because the clans had a sharp desire for independence. While he was considered king, something like this, where he showed weakness, could topple him. All that was known by the clan chiefs about the monks was they had entered a contract with them. Not one of them knew that Justin had simply acted as a go-between for them. Given the number of men that he was told the emperor could send, Justin was forced to agree to almost everything they wanted.

Justin finally decided that Solara needed to know that there were larger forces in his vicinity so he would be aware that his ally was watching. He knew that if he were going to attack the monks, it had best be done now while they were in separate war bands, as that would give Clayton the best chance to survive.

Focused on a course of action, Justin thought about the clan chiefs. Who would be most likely to accept the order?

It wouldn't matter though because all he wanted was cavalry to ride along whatever course Solara and Clayton would to meet up with other groups.

He didn't have enough time to send more than enough for Solara's group, so he would just make sure there was an overwhelming presence which would get his point across, he felt.

CHAPTER TWENTY-FOUR

Tom was about as exasperated at George as he could be. They were nowhere near to being free of the press of attackers in Clendenin and Tom could not get him to do what he wanted to, so they would have a chance of surviving the onslaught. The catapult had really hurt the outpost and the advance of the monks was enough to make him decide it was time to get George out.

The men King Simon had sent with George were probably the worst that he had ever seen. It was embarrassing the way they were pushed back into the outpost until there was no place for them to go but down to the ground from the advancing spears that stolidly advanced. Tom would not have thought that anyone would be able to penetrate the walls so quickly, or run their men into the ground so easily.

There was more to these monks than he first thought. He had never dealt with them personally and he could see by the group that ran through the outpost that they were serious about what they were doing, and practiced. It made him think that King Simon really had his work cut out for him by the disciplined pace of the formations advance the monks used to penetrate the walls.

It was uncanny. Tom knew he had been affected by that performance even as he, George, Sam, and John all made their escape with Tom's band as they were George's refuge.

Angling everyone to travel in the direction of the next outpost would mean keeping an outlook for any outliers from the rest of their army. That meant everyone was aware of their surroundings. George was firmly paying attention and had slipped into place nicely. Tom knew Clendenin was the most defensive outpost they had and to reach the closest one would be two days of travel by foot in hostile territory. That was a dangerous situation to be in under any condition. Just having escaped a siege would make anyone liven up.

There was a magnetic energy to the monks advance at Clendenin, and it was almost as if their formation carried an aura with it. It just brought with it a sense of dread of what was approaching as death itself was reaching out to you.

Tom had seen it twice before in other battles with other enemies that left the exact same impression on him that Clendenin had. The best thing to do was just keep moving away in an orderly manner, and look for a safe spot. You could get your bearings then.

Tom was keeping a close eye on George through his subordinates as he knew George was not ready to see that kind of carnage on his first assignment with the army. It would surely make him realize the importance of planning ahead on future incursions.

It looked like there would be more incursions with the demonstration that he saw on display. Tom knew his own men would not withstand an attack like that. His belief Waverly Hall would not fall had been shattered. Not beyond repair, but it had been an eye opener.

King Simon would have to dig deep to protect Waverly Hall. They were small numbers today, but would increase with time. Hopefully not too quickly. Tom was concerned this group would travel quickly from outpost to outpost, destroying each one, but that was the nearest place to find an ally in this part of the country. Luckily Tom had his men with him and knew what they were capable of.

He did see a good rate of survival for his band and George. The first few hours were critical to get away as far as possible, safely, then congregate and see who made it. It was common knowledge among his own men and George would see firsthand how important it was. That would make a man of him if he survived.

In cases like this it was what you knew that would see you through. It wouldn't do to lean on others until you were far enough away to be out of their loop, and Tom would decide when that would be. It was mostly grassland and forest in this area so he directed them to the tree line where they would have some cover, but not be encumbered by the brush among the trees.

It was basically more marching, is all. You had to put out of mind what just happened so that you were in the "hear and now" as you progressed to the next destination. That was one good aspect of a long march. You just could not be complacent, though the rhythm and sounds of a march could put you to sleep. You started one place and then suddenly you were someplace else.

John and a few other scouts had run ahead of the band to find a clear path to the outpost. Tom doubted they would cross anyone's path, but it gave the boys something to do, and everyone else a little confidence knowing there was a screen ahead to give them a warning, if they spotted the enemy.

Keeping a good pace, Tom looked around to see that each man had his weapons, water, and a pack with some food. That was a requirement with as much marching as they did. With the leather mail they wore it would not get too heavy on a march. Being a light infantry band was advantageous in an emergency. One never knew when the unexpected might arise.

The day was slightly warm. The snows had melted off except in the highest reaches. It made for good marching weather regardless of the reason for the march. Trying to put the recent loss in battle behind him, to blur out the memory of the carnage he witnessed, during the defense of Clendenin. That was more than enough reason.

It was just a defense mechanism Tom had learned over the years to keep himself alert until he found relative safety again. There were nights that it all came back to him but it was usually when he was safe somewhere and relaxed enough to think about it. Those were tough times but it reminded him that he was still living and he usually learned something.

He knew he was going to have to talk to George and he wasn't looking forward to it. There really wasn't much to say. He decided to wait until that eve before they made camp. He wasn't sure what he wanted to

                                         To Knew Beginnings Veil of Shadows

say other than his men were all here, but he would handle things until they reached the next outpost.

Deciding to pick up the pace, he motioned to those in view to go faster, so they would be further along when night set in. There wouldn't be a fire tonight with winter having passed, and even though the days were getting longer, it was still cold enough to see your breath before morn.

That might be a good time to wake George and shore him up. He needed to be reminded to stay upbeat for the men and know that help would be there when they reached the next outpost. He was looking a little sluggish, but the sun was setting and everyone was worn.

Motioning for a stop, Tom pointed to a copse aways ahead in the forest, where they could sleep for the night. It would have to be in shifts, as noise would travel freely in the dark. There was not going to be a moon either.

John was heading to the copse and Tom knew after he passed through there would either be a safe place to camp or he would motion everyone on. It wasn't long and he saw a few of the men follow John and knew it would be a safe refuge for the night. For them all.

It was a relief to get settled in the copse once sentries were set. Tom decided to get up early as there were scouts on the lookout. He wanted to slip over and catch George before anything happened.

Telling George that they would quietly break camp, he was interrupted by the sounds of dead leaves rustling from running footsteps.

Stopping mid-sentence, Tom motioned for George to relax, Tom closed his eyes and knew it was one of John's, probably with warning of attack. Sure enough, he ran right up to Tom and said, "They're searching for us."

Tom nodded and pushed the boy off while he made the decision to break camp.

Grabbing George by the shoulders, Tom told him to quietly start rustlin' everyone up. He knew George heard that they were being hunted, but he held up well without shock or fear in his eyes. He probably thought they would ransom him or something, but Tom could tell by the attack yesterday there was no chance anyone would go home alive if they resisted what was coming.

Tom started feeling fear in his chest, thinking about that, and he decided to try to keep everyone's mind off of it. Especially his.

As people started waking up things started to happen fast. Tom knew he stood no chance without a group of men to stand with so he headed in the direction that George went because he knew that would be his first priority in King Simon's eyes. Right now, Tom just felt the need to move his legs because he knew things were about to get bad. He could hear an occasional grunt, and feet running just to the south of his position, and he needed to go west to his destination. Tom knew they were going to be overrun.

He had to find George. Some of his men were forming up and there was nothing for it but to huddle up with 'em. They mostly had their weaponry, but not many shields. The first glint of metal advancing softly in the morning mist made it all too real. Whoever it was had been running, but now he just heard the cascade of marching feet and saw the glint of

To Knew Beginnings Veil of Shadows

sharp steel extended through the murky darkness. The way the spear tips led the way he could see that they knew exactly where everyone stood.

Rather than put up a fruitless resistance, and because he didn't see George, he dropped his weapons and told his men to stand down. Yeah, they could take some of them out but he knew they would be the worse for it. One of the men took note and stopped the formation from advancing.

Tom heard him say something, some kind of gobbledy gook, and he just squatted down and let out a deep breath. For some reason the fear just intensified in him until he couldn't move, but just went to his hands and knees and said, "I repent."

The soldier that had stopped the formations advance peeled away from his men and strode confidently forward. Tom felt the urge to look up, and it was like he had come under this stranger's control.

"It was him."

Tom hung his head again as the weight seemed to lift from his body and he went to his hands and knees with weakness.

This went well beyond anything that he had experienced, and even then it was still worse than he expected. The only thing that Tom could think was this man came from Emperor Ishima.

"George is dead. You should have killed my man the other day when you caught him. He was too close but, now he is dead, when I found out you (HAD SEEN HIM).

The words seemed to shimmer through the air with a force that captivated Tom and all of his senses and just left him feeling so relieved inside. It was almost as if nothing ever existed when this man spoke, and he was now a true believer. For just a moment the old Tom spoke, and said,

"This is some weird sorcery or something," but then he laughed and said, "No, this is life."

CHAPTER TWENTY-FIVE

Solara finally felt like she was letting loose the might of the monks on a new land. A small detachment of hers had tracked down a band of men that somehow had the prince of Waverly Hall. She was disappointed that he had been killed during the capture, but really didn't care, because that was their final destination.

There was a man named Tom that ordered the surrender of his men. Some of his men were killed before that happened, but he didn't seem to have any resentment for that. He actually seemed so impressed by his capture that he wanted to side with the monks.

She found that amusing, but useful, though she hadn't decided what she wanted to do with him yet. It would be beneficial to have a small war band such as his working from the inside. She didn't trust sending Tom back to the king, though, since he had just lost his son.

It would wait for another day, and she had just said to treat them like honored prisoners. That way they would be fed and watered, not mistreated, though they would have no luxuries.

The cleanup of Clendenin had been performed successfully. She was proud of the way Clayton handled the rest of the prisoners and they would not be seen again. She was waiting for her first report from the other outposts. She felt sure they would have been taken with just three thousand monks on standby.

She realized that they were going to be leaving several piles of bone that would disintegrate into dust by the end of summer if they left them on the ground. It would prove as a reminder for anyone who dared to protest. Each outpost could be a warning if things went as planned.

Waiting patiently for any kind of report on the other attacks, Solara decided to walk amongst her men and see what the mood was. Everyone knew there would be reports, and they had all enjoyed the taking of Clendenin, but she wanted to remind them there was work yet to be done, and her presence should remind them of that, and settle their nerves.

It was a slow walk through camp. The men looked at her and she knew they were seeing a man. Depending on how the reports panned out she decided she was ready to reveal herself. There was something about all of the Terlingua monks that made them susceptible to the person with the strongest will, and Emperor Ishima had chosen her for just that purpose. Someone as strong as her should lead from the front, he had told her, and she had.

His belief in her system of attack and command pleased him greatly, he had said, before they had agreed that she would be the first spear in this new attack, on a new land. Now that they were on foot, everyone would pack their spears, and carry swords again, as they advanced through the countryside.

Solara had no fear or worry about the outcome of the other outposts. Clayton's men had performed shamelessly, and she had intervened simply to speed things up, and save lives.

She had lost a few men herself, and they had been honored, traditionally, as the first sacrifices of this new land.

She had been paying close attention to features of the landscape and found it all pleasing to the eye.

She could actually picture raising a family here, and hoped to bring settlers just for that. Home was crowded. Being in command of a unit set her free in a way that few others experienced. It was humbling, and when she thought of Emperor Ishima, she hoped to provide an acceptable conquest of Waverly Hall at his feet.

She wasn't ready to say that she was going to do away with Hasson Heights as well, though, and was unsure that her performance was too anticipatory. She wanted to please and may have overreacted. She would temper herself more fully in the future. That is what the emperor would say.

Don't show too much, she reminded herself. The emperor had never turned his full attention to the mainland and she was quite sure the mainlanders were not aware of their ancient abilities.

All Solara would have to do is whisper fright to key members of her men. They would spread the word carefully throughout, and the aura projected turned the spears a very pretty bright blue that you could only see when the spears turned towards you. It was a sight Solara never grew tired of.

Emperor Ishima must be told that their basic tenet worked perfectly. Fright, just fright.

Solara felt a swelling in her chest of pride towards being a commander. Her men would not suffer too greatly during this campaign and it was going to be a long one. She remembered the first battle she was an officer in, dressed as a man, walking from one end of the battlefield, to the other, which took a full day.

It was a security safety that she had suggested. With her aura she could tame and subdue her fellow soldiers just by passing through. There were picked men following her through the crowd and she was able to cast her vision to them. If she sent something, even without thinking about it, there was always someone to investigate what had caught her eye.

In time she had begun to achieve a reputation as someone who could calm a situation. Discipline of the men grew, as she, dressed as a man, almost became invisible because with time they were all picked men. Just because she hadn't noticed them. That's when the change happened. Instead of casting people off she began pulling people in. Like gravity.

People that had never seen her before could never remember what she looked like, and just remembered a slight man that could glide. It made them protective. She fostered that, and pulled it all in, until she was standing at the head of the army.

That slim figure most men could barely remember was respected because they knew that although he was small, he was fast as lightning. That is how she had earned her way.

There were so many secret ways in battle for Terlingua. It was a true travesty the destruction of their own kind when the wars at home were spreading. It was so much better to have a foreign enemy.

There was not much left to do around Clendenin as they had salted the land. It would be a blight, a stark reminder, of who was invaded first. The salt would leech into the land and spread into the wells they drew their water from, and no one would live there again.

The fallen had been stacked in a triangle, as he had requested, and she was proud of Clayton for that display. The bones would stay, as that is what she wanted to leave behind.

CHAPTER TWENTY-SIX

King Simon was pissed!

That fool Clayton had somehow killed George and captured Tom and his men.

He was lucky to even have a report, but Tom had seen to that. Tom was lucky because he knew Tom was still with him. Simon didn't know if he would stay his man, but believed he would. They had discussed this years ago when they had first met, and Tom said he would remember that he was "my man" and would stay faithful.

That was the hard part to understand.

That was going to be put to the test. Simon kicked a few loose pebbles that was where they shouldn't be. He kicked them both and missed one. That was George, he thought. Just sitting there while Tom was sent off in the distance.

Simon decided that he would not check on Tom with George dead... There would be so many gobbledy gook formalities. He wished he'd never had George. His only son. That was so disappointing to him.

He would observe the formalities, but would not ask for the remains. It just wasn't worth the trouble.

So, what to do now. He had sent George with Tom, even though he and George did not get along. Simon thought Tom would sort him out one way or another. The attack seems to have been overwhelming.

Tom must have seen something in George that he did not like. Simon had to admit that he couldn't blame him. The hurt must show though. It wouldn't totally be an act. George had been off a little though, and Tom gave Simon a chance to see to that.

He wasn't sure if George were right or wrong in whatever those two had gotten mixed up in. He had reached out himself to the monks to find exactly what Hasson Heights plans were. He wasn't totally convinced that an overwhelming army of monks would be attacking him soon.

It would be today, or tomorrow, but, if you were interested, we could corral all of Clayton's for you to dispose of. The only catch is you must do it in battle. Solara was a woman, and she would command.

That put prickles up Simon's back that made him want to get a sword and put an end to both of these aggressors. The more he thought about it, the more it made him want to spar. Nothing complicated, he just wanted something to hit. So, after that, he would reach out and see where all of his men were, determine where the enemy was and begin to make a war plan.

Solara's attack had been an instruction of how well behaved her men were, and willing to follow any command. Given by her. Not any of her men.

A threat from a foreign woman aggressor. Swordplay was in Simon's blood, and he thought he may have just found a new victim. Simon did not care whether it was woman, child, or man, that he killed, just so he could abate this blood thirst of being attacked unprepared.

With the loss of George, Simon wouldn't miss him. With that train of thought snuffed out, Simon began thinking about who he would need to fill George's place. That would be more of a communication issue than a fighting one, which would make things easier for Simon to control once the communication issue was hocked up.

He may just start getting in touch to the commander of the Waverly Hall Regulars, Chuck Downs, as it seemed apparent that this "Solara" was intent on destroying whoever she came into contact with.

There was no word of Clayton, but if something were to happen to him, he would have heard. He would have to follow up on that.

His cousin Phillip could contact Lucas Bellway, since he was in charge of the Pine Hall Financial Mint. He could convey the soldiers pay, and hope for no disruptions.

Food, supplies, and weapons were accounted for. He wasn't ready to lead the regulars, and wanted to see how they performed. They were indentured servants to the military that would never see their freedom.

They were allowed to mate, though, and their sons and daughters made up the main forces that he put under his command. It was just rough young men as the first freed generation, year after year.

Some of the older generations had lasted long enough to reach high stations of command. Those they could bleed off at any point. The matter of numbers was something that worried him. He had it repeated to him from someone he didn't know that the monks were sending just a small group to test the defenses on the continent.

And they had started with him.

That said a lot in itself. He knew he was being double crossed, but until he knew the full account of the monk's numbers, after they had landed, he would marshal his forces and roll the dice on one battle. If he lost, it would have been a battle to prevent his extinction. That is the message he read in the bones left behind by "Solara." Clayton had reported that she had gone too far, though he was not supposed to know that.

He did not have the manpower to block off the coast. Not even for part of the coast. There was nothing for it but to accept the fact that the monks were invading and there was nothing he could do to stop them. Except hope to beat them in the field.

That would be a true test. That was the quandary he was in right now, and trying to work through any extraneous issues before he devoted himself to war. Solara was a competent leader, and had proven the tenacity of her men as soon as they were engaged and, unfortunately, he was impressed. He just got a feeling that this would be a good chance to test her abilities.

He had not led in the field for several years, and missed the concentration to root through all of the possibilities in times of war. There wouldn't be any hostages, or swaps. There would be no ransoms. No one would contact the so-called King Justin.

If this was his doing, Simon would see to the man himself. He knew what happened to Jonas Weaver, even though he had disappeared, and that would have been a pleasant way to go if Simon got his hands on Justin. It was just as well because Simon was still hale enough to enjoy a good march, and, a fight.

The city guard would see to any mishaps while he was gone and make sure there was no sheltering the enemy. He would allow them to close the city off, if needed, or if he gave the order himself.

Tom should have two men off in the distance. He normally would. If so, he would need to go to the shock tower. That's where the archers would be and Tom had said he would send two as that would be all he could spare.

Simon knew that if he was not able to convince the monks to take over Hasson Heights, that he would lose to two enemies. That was just inevitable, as he would be hard pressed to just handle Justin. He felt he could. Waverly Hall wasn't dominant for no reason.

While pondering, Simon heard footsteps at the entrance of shock tower. He stopped, waiting to see who it would be. He didn't recognize the man, but a hand motion was all he needed to, so he followed him.

Catching up to him, he looked worse for wear, but healthy, and he knew he was one of Tom's.

"King Simon,…"

Simon shook his head, reaching out to steady the scout, "Welcome back John, I'd hoped you'd made it. Did Tom get you out?"

John laughed, and said, "He did, but George didn't make it."

King Simon grinned, saying, "Yes, I've heard. What Was Tom's prediction?"

That's when John's head bobbed and he looked to the side and said, "It's hopeless. I watched Tom surrender and he looked terrified. It was unnatural."

King Simon could feel the fright, in waves, pouring off the man,. It took a few moments for it to dissipate, and Simon shook his head, saying, "Since Tom said…."

"No, you don't understand.."

"It doesn't matter if I understand, it still has to be done."

That was when John snapped out of it.

"Something strange is happening." Simon said.

CHAPTER TWENTY-SEVEN

Clayton had been relegated to messenger. Solara had captured a band of men and their leader Tom had become the focus of attention.

Clayton was going to see firsthand how well the other outposts fared. He would bring everyone back to Clendenin. There would be a guard at each outpost, but that was all.

Solara wanted Clendenin to be her command post and was already jockeying to be top commander. That was scary to Clayton, and if she wasn't, there would be someone even more qualified, and he didn't dare think on that.

He would have to round up his men quietly so they could have a meeting.

It was a long haul to reach all of the outposts, but Clayton knew he needed the time, and Solara would need the time as well to position herself to refortify Clendenin. She was rebuilding the walls already. The bad part of that is she would be camped as near Hasson Heights as she could be and still have a structure to defend with. Clayton was going to have to make a connection with his father, and that shouldn't be a problem as they were all allies for the moment.

Each outpost had been stationed equidistant from each other. That, at least, gave him the chance to plan between stops, as he saw what happened to each one. He was not in doubt that his men were able to take the other outposts. He just hoped the other bands of monks were not as aggressive as what he had seen from Solara's forces.

He was traveling with four other men on horseback. If they were caught unawares they would be able to outrun any pursuit if things didn't go their way. Mainly Clayton just wanted to keep the peace. He was impressed with Solara's men, but his own men were just as good.

He could see a clearance up ahead and saw a rider approaching. It was easy to see that the man was one of his officers, by the quality of horse he rode, and his bearing.

Motioning to the rider, the man turned in his direction, sped into a trot, until close enough to be heard.

"Sir," the man said, "I've been on my way to meet you for two days. I was at the furthest outpost, Crocodile. There were no defenders by the time we occupied the outpost."

"It was the strangest thing." He continued, "We never could determine where they went. It's like they just disappeared."

Clayton's mind went blank.

"Were there tunnels?"

"If there were we didn't see them. We were quick, but thorough. Now I'm worried."

"No need," Clayton quipped, "from what we left behind, if there were a way for them to leave, Commander Solara will soon know. How have our forces interacted with the monks?"

"There really hasn't been any interaction. We have developed a simple hand signal for marching and formations, just so we know where each other stand, but no one speaks the language."

Clayton wasn't surprised, but hadn't thought about it being a problem for the other groups of men at the other outposts. He had been focused mainly on positioning everyone correctly and not so much on who told everyone what the comradery would be between the groups.

Clayton was a little surprised to see that someone had traveled this far since the attacks. His sense of time had faded since Clendenin, as there had been so much to do. There was always Solara, too. Clayton had gotten around the fact that Solara was not a man, but had sent word to his father, and expected a change of heart in his father's outlook on the contributions of his allies.

The rider moved on. Apparently with something else on his mind. It was good to know their furthest end was occupied by his men. He would have to find out more if he saw anyone else before they arrived at the next outpost.

Solara said there had been someone named Tom that she had captured, and she would allow Clayton to question him, with conditions. He didn't know what those conditions were, but it couldn't hurt to question the man.

He would do that in the dark beside a fire to encourage him to speak the truth. If he truly had changed sides he would have to prove it.

Clayton had heard of a group in George's employ, but had never seen them, so he wouldn't recognize them on sight. With George dead they may just want a new employer, but he doubted Solara would be interested in paying. Their armor and weapons spoke of a well-equipped company of men that stuck together.

He had sent a message to his father when he had finished cleaning up the aftermath at Clendenin. He expected some type of help from the clans, but didn't know who would call men to arms or if his father would use more of their own. He hoped it would be the other clans providing the men so they would have enough protection at home in the event of a surprise attack.

It wasn't long before the unknown rider returned with something on his mind.

"Sir, I wanted to look at your men. It seems this is the only group of monks who took the field out of the four assembled groups. Also, so you know, your father has called up a veritable army of light cavalry scouts and skirmishers to watch everyone. Even if they are in sight they will not be reachable. That should give everyone something to think of."

Clayton thought about that for a moment wondering if it was a good idea or not. Finally, he said, "That is bold. If you can get a message to them for me it would be of great help."

"That shouldn't be a problem. You're the only one who knows they are out there. It would be easy to send a message to your father. I am sure he would appreciate regular reports until he decides how much heavy cavalry he wants to send. I'd say it will be a considerable amount."

"It needs to be. From what I have seen of Solara's men, it wouldn't hurt for the monks to see that there is a check in place, so they do not grow too brazen. It would help everyone to know they are there. It would be good for morale."

The rider stayed silent and motionless. Clayton was somewhat surprised that he didn't recognize the man. As easily as he had worked his way through their lines he know that the man was familiar with how he maintained discipline and focus. Anyone could be shocked by what they had seen and knowing there was a force within striking distance as support would really make a difference.

Clayton was about to ask him who he was when a commotion started off in the distance, Grabbing his attention.

"How long will you be with us?"

"As long as you need. I can take a message that will be relayed to your father and have a response in just a couple of days."

Clayton thought it a good idea to have a line of communication between him and his dad, as they were really the only two who knew what was happening with a contract with Terlingua. He wasn't sure if his father was being open with him about the purpose of the attacks planned by Terlingua. Something just seemed off, though he couldn't place what.

"I need to see what all of the ruckus is about. We'll talk later and determine a way for us to communicate. It shouldn't be difficult, but I would like to keep it to our breast right now. The less who know, the better, until we see how things play out. I am sure there will be more additions to both of our ranks in the coming months and this battle has just barely begun. We are in for a long haul."

Clayton left the man to see what sounded like a fight with an audience taking place. It was one of Tom's men, who had been captured with him, squaring off against one of the short and stocky monks with short swords. Clayton did not know either man, and just going by their appearance, it looked to be a pretty even match.

Men from every corner had come to see the fight and it must have been something he had not heard about, and he should have. With nothing for it, Clayton shouldered his way forward until he could see the two combatants. Wagers being made were slowing down and the largest man Clayton had ever seen walked forward to start the death match.

Clayton couldn't believe they were going to put themselves at risk in the middle of a war. He couldn't comprehend why anyone would do that now. He started to make his way to the fighters but the large man that had separated the two fighters made his way around the crowd, making sure no one was too close, including Clayton.

Soon enough the man clapped two hands together that looked like hams and when he threw his hand down and backed out the two combatants began circling to the left with their swords in their right hands. Tom's man was wiry, which probably meant he was fast, while the monk was short and powerful. Clayton, forgetting about the loss of life about to happen, couldn't decide who he would bet on.

The fight was one of the strangest things that Clayton had ever seen. Someone nearby had said this was Waverly Hall's best fighter and Clayton didn't think it would take long as he didn't see how the brute force of the stocky monk would compare with the speed and agility of Tom's man, who looked contemptuous at the man before him.

Clayton was proven right immediately. Tom's man lunged forward blindingly fast, and the monk barely had time to move. Just a slight turn was all that was needed to dodge the strike of Tom's man. Clayton thought it was just luck.

This went on some time until it was proven that the monk was reacting, but in such small motions that he barely seemed to move. Almost in a trance, when the killing blow came Clayton didn't realize what happened at first. Somehow, even quicker than Tom's man, the monk shifted right, throwing the piercing sword to the left, and took the man's head off. It was so unexpected and quick that hardly anyone in the crowd knew what to think. Clayton was baffled momentarily, then recovered and grew a new respect for the sword master that had just put on a show of a mildness that was deadly.

Having never seen anything like it in the past, Clayton wondered just what all he would send in his missive to his father.

CHAPTER TWENTY-EIGHT

Toleo had been very busy since that first passage to the mainland. No one on the high seas would be able to come close to matching his power in the flotilla that he ferried soldiers with. His only problem was spring rain and storms that threatened to capsize even the largest of his ships.

He was bringing in the last of six transports, each with three thousand men apiece. They had moved ever inland as he brought them, and they had made a veritable city just beyond the cove where everyone disembarked. With so many idle hands Toleo had decided to expand the landing zone around the cove so unloading would be easier.

He wanted true houses built as well, and ditches and piping for sanitary use. Being so close to the ocean gave them a constant source of seawater that could be used for everything except drinking and cooking.

There were parties out digging wells since this was turning into a semi-permanent camp.

Even Toleo didn't know how many transports Emperor Ishima planned on sending, but this was definitely a good start. Emperor Ishima had a hundred thousand warriors in his personal retinue, and those men would be the last to be sent overseas, if they came at all. This could just be a lark on his part, for all he knew, as manpower was not something they were short of.

What was most needed was someone like Commander Solara. Totally dependable, educated and dedicated. He knew the emperor and Solara were familiar with each other from what seemed to be shared interests in some of the arcane histories that were kept private. There were other intimates of the emperor who shared a similar position, but Toleo suspected Solara was a rare talent in her field to be held in such high regard.

Toleo had passengered a quartet of sorcerers once, on his second sail as Master of the Fleet and it was an event he did not want to ever do again. As they were unofficially high-ranking government officials, Toleo had been inclined to place them with a less crowded ship than his own, but they were adamant that they sail with him on his own ship.

There was no argument that he could present to disway them, so he bowed and presented them his own quarters. Seemingly satisfied, Toleo thought no more of it until that night when he walked out on deck and saw them in some kind of strange séance that stood his hair on end. Terrified they would see him watching, he turned, just as they started chanting, and he ran back to his borrowed cabin.

　　　　　　　　　　To Knew Beginnings Veil of Shadows

When he got there his heart was pounding but it quickly subsided, and he felt foolish for being scared. Even now it was ludicrous to have reacted that way, but he never wanted to see it again. Something had been glowing in the darkness that the sorcerers were conjuring in and looked to be growing. He could not stand the memory of what little he saw, much less what was actually being performed.

It was something he put out of mind, but it just came back to him when he first saw the emperor and Solara together and the quiet talk they had.

He was sure she was mixed up in that somehow, but it was not his business, and he did not see or speak to anyone about it. Just to think about sharing made him feel like he would vomit from nausea.

Shaking his head to push the memory away, Toleo used quite a bit of self-control to master himself, and focus on the issue of Solara.

She was putting on a masterful performance. The drilling she required her men to perform had worked perfectly, according to Siris, who she had sent back as she knew he was a plant for Toleo.

That was no surprise to either of them, as anyone could get close to whoever they needed to and disappear without a trace.

Occasionally, both would disappear without a trace. There were so many machinations at court that one never truly knew who they were dealing with. Time was the true equalizer and would help build some type of trust. That could turn a stranger into an ally.

That is what he was trying to do with Solara.

Toleo's position as Master of the Fleet was uncontested, but he felt like he was limited by his performance in that others would not allow him to advance to court himself. It was like sailing into a wave so tall, and unpredictable, as to prevent any attempt of rescue or flight. He only wanted to be proud of his time in command, but with no one jockeying for his position, he didn't know how to advance his career.

Entering court life was a dream of many Terlinguan men and women. It wasn't often that even the most qualified of the candidates were given an exam for admission. What the exam consisted of was closely guarded. The only people who knew what it consisted of were the examiners and its victorious.

No one who passed the examination ever returned to tell the tale. You had to apply with no foreknowledge of what would be asked, and what it consisted of was sacrosanct, as all involved were not seen or heard from again.

The mystique around the examination was only compounded by the fact that there was always sorcerer's lurking in the shadows. There was a strange feeling of sanctity involved wherever they were. They did not speak to anyone who was not of their own kind, and no one was allowed to approach them for any reason.

They appeared well kept. You couldn't identify what sex they were because of the voluminous robes and trinkets they wore. With shaved heads and makeup, combined with the darkness that pervaded around them, you could only assume they were human and ancient.

Toleo was under watch. He didn't know who, or where in the fleet, that person, or persons would be, but he knew they were put there. It was routine, but with forces being ferried back and forth, so quickly, Toleo was on edge.

He was well protected by his own men, and he wasn't defenseless. Some attempts were simply unable to be stopped. Once you accepted that, you just relaxed. It could happen at any time, just like with anything else.

CHAPTER TWENTY-NINE

With no body, the ceremony was bereft of the true spirit of defeat that King Simon had suffered with the loss of his eldest child. George was gone, and he didn't even know where the body was.

The new heir apparent, Henry, now the eldest son, had been called in from duty to see what arrangements needed to be made with the loss of the former heir apparent. He had been training in the field as a page. Simon didn't want Heny to turn out like George, so he sent him off at just seven years old.

There was no chance Henry would be like George. The first thing Henry was assigned to was cleaning the latrines. If he was going to command, and he was, then the first lesson he should learn was how to care for the health of his soldiers.

 To Knew Beginnings Veil of Shadows

Yes, Henry was going to be trained from the ground up and would not be given the chance to be as disrespectful and careless as George had been. Simon was going to see to that personally. His heir would have to know everything about his troops and everything it took to keep them in the field. Mainly keeping the treasury in action to pay the troops.

Simon was able to have some professional soldiers, along with the regulars, and he would keep them as close to home as he could until he knew better how things turned out with the new threat in the field.

Four outposts had been taken on the same day, which showed Solara's determination to win. She was trying to use intimidation by orchestrating four attacks in one day that were successful. That was just boastful to Simon. A personal challenge, and by now she had had Tom long enough to pump him for valuable information, and that was scary. Tom knew way too much.

It couldn't be helped, though. What was done, was done. This farce of a ceremony was almost through. As soon as he left he was going to round up some replacements to send until he was able to form up the regulars himself. Then he would put them in the van and lead them from the rear.

The city was stock full of defenders, and those in the nearby countryside, and he was comfortable with leaving it to someone else while he stepped out with the army. It felt like a good time to go for a stroll with some of his own retainers to see how that would go.

With the ceremony finally over, Simon stepped out as quietly as he could so as not to make a scene. Most likely Justin would have people in place to report back Simon's movements. Marshalling an army would definitely raise some eyebrows.

Simon realized he was upset about George's death. Simon had been too busy to pay much attention to him as he grew. He had been a sweet boy, but the man had been ruined. Simon would not make the same mistake with Henry.

He had no idea how many of the enemy were in the field. Getting back on track after the ceremony was making him ill. That and the thought of going back into the field.

He loved to fight. He was almost ecstatic with a reason to go back. There was dread as well. It did provide relief to know he wouldn't have to rely on George. Tom was difficult to lose, though.

His chest tightened at the thought.

Tom had been so reliable…

Now he would have to rely on Chuck Downs. He was the commander in Emerald Bay.

Chuck was his niece's husband and kept things in order very well. Simon doubted Chuck had enough men on hand to wipe these marauders out, but could be a real hindrance to further progress in the free movement they had been enjoying. If he could get that to stop he would be well ahead.

They would have to advance through East Lake. That would put them closer to the capital than he liked, but it would draw them in as well.

If Chuck could get their army to stop, it would give him time to get the regulars on their feet and in position to make them sound the retreat. If he could keep Chuck in place, he would be able to surround the enemy.

If he could wait them out he would. Chuck would have to make sure the supply lines stayed active, else he would have to release them from their acting duty.

He would have to speak with Isabel, as well. She wouldn't mourn George, but she would appreciate that their sons, Lester and James, were that much closer to the throne.

Simon was on his third wife, and the connection to the past wouldn't be missed. George had been his first, by Simone. His father had thought Simon marrying a woman named Simone would prove sound. It had, and was a happy and prosperous marriage.

She had died giving birth to Valerie, that was his second child, first daughter, who was now betrothed to Robert Blake.

Robert was a wonderful artificer who could make an infusion to the treasury to see him off to a good start. He was well acquainted with security measures and had merchant lines that could help shore up any deficiencies to mobilize the army.

Working through his thoughts, Simon started piecing together a plan to win the field and regain control of all four outposts.

He would mobilize an army large enough to invade Hasson Height's as well.

CHAPTER THIRTY

Hayden was afraid the trip north was not going as planned. He was scared C.C. was going to suffer needlessly, and he could not do anything to prevent it. They were in a rut, two of the wagons that is. It was raining and everything was soaked.

He had finally had C.C.'s pavilion built and watched a good bit of the camp constructed. A river crossing had partially collapsed, and it would be a few days before they had repaired it.

Hayden himself was soaked, and he had barely stepped out in the rain. It was probably a good thing that the bridge had collapsed, because it gave them the chance to dig in and rest for a couple of days, as everyone was tired.

C.C. would need a fire and hot drink before the evening was over. He had taken her father's advice and packed extra soft, heavy, blankets for just such an occasion.

Her father had warned him that it may come to this as she did not travel well and would need luxury for the entire trip. He agreed totally and was determined that she not suffer any hardship, despite conditions.

It had been a horrible day traveling. Most of the camp had been started that morning and they only had to travel half the day to make it to rest and safety. There hadn't been any trouble on the journey, but with the rumors of war in the air, Hayden didn't trust anybody that wasn't a part of the original travelers from The Cinder's Party, as they had traveled with others, and some had already departed.

It would be another ten days before they reached Lower Grand, and Hayden and C.C. would turn northeast to travel on to Hasson Heights. No one had received a response to Hayden's inquiry for marriage, but decided to make the trip regardless. C.C. had been in a fine mood the past week. It seemed like being on the road was good for her.

There had been some kind of fighting, but Hayden was just going off of rumors that he had heard while traveling. Hayden didn't know if Clayton would be available when they arrived. He would have to inquire about Clayton's father, King Justin.

He and C.C. had talked quite a bit on the journey. She was very charming now that they were friends. She had talked about her brother, Smoke, quite a bit as he was a fine craftsman of iron. She had even brought along a few examples of his work to show the king.

A good night's rest would help everyone.

Thinking back, Hayden couldn't conceive how he had thought of C.C. as shrewish. She was simply amazing, and he knew that he was putty in her hands. She made him feel as if that were right and just. He enjoyed the feeling. Helping a damsel was perfect for his constitution and gave him something to focus on.

There was talk of battles being fought in East Lake, but nothing had interfered with their journey so far. It was amazing not to be teaching. The weather had been wonderful to boot.

King Justin was going to be surprised to see them this summer. Lack of heat from the desert made for a cool night this far north. He may have to change clothes and get his own heavy blankets.

With the rain finally letting up, and a smell of mud in the air, Hayden worried. It was nothing he wanted C.C. to see, but she could be walking into a funeral as much as a wedding. If outposts had been taken in East Lake that would be a huge surprise to start a war. Justin may be out in the field as well. If he and Clayton were out fighting for their lives, well, he and C.C. would have to stay and see it through.